**Clint Faraday**
book 46
*Dead Man's Moon*

Clint is in Chiriqui Grande for supplies. It is moonrise, a beautiful golden full moon – with a small red spot.

Osorio says it is the dead man's moon because of that red spot.

It turns out it really was!

# Contents

# About the author

CD Moulton has traveled extensively over much of the world both in the music business, where he was a rock guitarist, songwriter and arranger and in an import/export business. He has been everything from a bar owner to auto salvage (junkyard) manager, longshoreman to high steel worker, orchid grower to landscaper, tropical fish farmer to commercial fisherman. He started writing books in 1983 and has published more than 350 books as of January 1, 2023. His most popular books to date are about research with orchids, though much of his science fiction and fantasy work has proven popular. He wrote the CD Grimes, PI series, and the Det. Nick Storie series, Clint Faraday series, and many other works.

He now resides in Gualaca, Chiriqui, Panamá, where he writes books, plays music with friends, does research with orchids and medicinal plants. He has lately become involved in fighting for the rights of the indigenous people, who are among his closest friends, and in fighting the extreme corruption in the courts and police in Panamá.

He offers the free e-book, *Fading Paradise*, that explains what he has been through because of the corruption.

CD is the discoverer of the Chadam Protocol for curing cancer.

Facebook page Ambrosia peruviana for cancer.

## Dead Man's Moon

### *Beyond Beautiful*

"Clint! Jantoro deo!" Osorio Rincón, Indigeno friend called as Clint was putting the supplies he'd bought into his steel lockbox on his boat. "Are you staying here tonight?"

"Yeah," Clint Faraday, retired PI from Florida, now living here in Panamá, where he had been declared a Ngobe Indio by the council. He had a family, a beautiful wife and a son and daughter. Tyna was a Ngobe by birth. His two children, Clintonito (Nito), 7 years old, and Nicole, 6 years old were being raised on the comarca in the Indio tradition. "It's getting dark. I'll wait until morning to go to Cusapín."

"It's a full moon. It won't be dark on the water. We'd still like for you to stay to trade tales and lies."

Clint laughed and said he was staying. He would be at Jorge's house after a few beers and some better lies than Osorio and his friends could possibly think up.

"I don't have time to lie. Those five young sexy

women who won't leave me alone see to it I don't have time to make up stories."

"Except the one you made up with them in it," Clint fired back. Osorio gave him the bird and they headed for the cantina, laughing and joking. They got beers and joined four other Indigenos on the deck over the Caribbean. The moon was just peeking across the mountains on the other side of the harbor. They watched as it rose to a few degrees above the mountain tops. Clint said it was beautiful beyond belief with the reflections on the wave tips.

"Oh, damn! It's a dead man's moon!" Osorio suddenly cried. The others nodded. There was a red spot on the lower left side of the moon. Clint knew it was because of a small cloud with a prism effect at just that angle. It would fade in a few minutes at most. The Indigenos had an uncanny sense of almost psychic power about such things. He'd seen the tribe elders make predictions and explain omens in sunsets and moonrises before. They were almost never wrong in their readings. Some, such as this, would often seem to be predictions because someone they would hear about would die during the night. Someone died in the comarca almost every night. If it was someone nearby, they could claim it was predicted.

"Murder," Enrique predicted. "It is the color of blood. Someone will die tonight by the knife."

That would restrict the prediction. Enrique was very positive about it.

They discussed a couple of times when the dead man's moon made a prediction and it came true. Enrique told of when Fernando Something-or-other fell off a ledge and hit his head on a rock and died. The dead man's moon spot was more brown than red, which meant he would die by being hit with a rock. The prediction wasn't close enough that him hitting the rock or vice versa would be the case.

They soon talked of other things. Clint went to bed about one o'clock in the morning. He didn't drink much beer in Cusapín so the four he had did relax him enough that he slept well

In the morning he bought a few more items and headed for home and family. He had to wait for a small intense rain, then was gone.

<u>*Right Again!*</u>

When Clint pulled into the dock at Cusapín there were a number of people gathered around the little shed where the fishing gear was stored by the fishermen. Neto saw him coming to the dock and called him to the shed. There was blood all over the place. Basilio had been called and would be there in a few minutes. There was a lot of blood. Somebody was hurt. Bad. They didn't know who.

Clint looked at the blood carefully. It was congealed enough that he could say it had been left there more than two hours ago, considering the high humidity level.

That much blood? Whoever would be dead by now if they hadn't gotten a transfusion!

The rain had moved east before him. It had just stopped here. The shed was by the dock on the beach end.

Clint went to carefully look at the beach sand. There was a slightest tint of pink in spots. He called that whoever it was had run down the beach. They went as a group, following the few other pinkish spots they discovered. There was a big mestizo man's body by a little patch of heavy scrub at the edge of the beach.

The pinkish patches were at the water line. He had run in the edge of the water.

Clint studied the sand between the water and that spot. There wasn't much color. The sand was deeply imprinted.

"He was dead and was carried to here," Clint said. "He's pretty big. It wasn't a small person who dumped him.

"Will someone please go to Basilio? This will need his authority." Rigo nodded and headed back to the town. They waited for about ten minutes. He returned to say that Clint was in charge and was acting with the request of the council. Basilio had to go into the comarca to settle a few things among the people at the Rio Cañas settlement as to how repairs were to be made to the community house. An old tree had fallen and badly damaged the roof. Basilio would appoint someone to oversee the repairs and would be back the following day. Until he returned Clint was to be treated as the jefe.

Clint sighed. At least this was his line of work He could handle it.

They turned the body over. There were deep stab wounds in the stomach and upper leg.

"He was stabbed and ran for the water. He was followed and dropped somewhere fairly close to the shed. He bled out fast with that leg wound. It cut an artery.

"Have any of you seen him before?"

Nando said, "His name was Ernesto Guevarra. He came with three others yesterday late in a boat. They are staying at the pensión. Ariela and Samuél Acosta and Maria Benito."

"Have they been here before?"

"Only Maria. She was with some gringos two months ago for a day and night. Jerry and Donna Franklin. From Wisconsin in the EE. UU. She told them about our town and told them they would like it here."

Nando was night clerk at the pensión. He knew a lot and had a very good memory.

"Yes. I spent the night with Maria then," Arturo said. "She wanted to have some experience with an Indio and said she couldn't get away with it where she lived in Clayton. They are against the Indios there. I did not know she was anyone's novia at the first. She told me when she left that I was so much better than her novio she couldn't believe it."

"She is the very sexy and pretty older lady whose father is from Colombia?" Chino asked. "She asked me where you were and I told her you were out working with the nispero."

"I saw this one last night. He came to the dock to

ask where Arturo was. I told him probably in the mountains because you were working with the madera," Tonio said. "He was a very angry man."

"Why did you kill him, Arturo?" Clint asked.

"He tried to kill me," Arturo answered after a moment. "He said I raped his wife and she was pregnant and I was going to pay for it.. He sent Celio for me in the mountains. I told him she wasn't pregnant by me because we used the thing Dave gave me to be sure there were no children. He tried to stick me with his knife. I took it away from him and he tried to choke me. I stuck him, then took him here."

Clint sat on a stump and thought. "We have to find out what's going on here. First thing is to find if Maria's pregnant. If she brought them here, there was something ... we have to know. Neem is one hundred percent as a contraceptive.

"Arturo, you should have reported it to Basilio. You shouldn't have brought the body here."

"I didn't want her to know about it yet. I wanted to talk to her and ask why she said I raped her. I thought the rain would take the blood away and you wouldn't find him for a day here."

Clint nodded.

"How did you know it was me?"

"You're the only one here big enough to carry him that far." Arturo nodded.

"Somebody get a tarp from the shed and take his body to the clinic," Clint said. "I want somebody to see Maria before I tell her her boyfriend's dead."

He went back along the beach to the town with Ernesto, who would take the tarp to them. Arturo would carry the body back. After all, he's the one who took it there.

Clint thought about how this would be handled in Florida and outside the comarca here. There would be fifty city cops and CSI and a ME crew swarming all over the place. It would take them a month to sort through the details to try to find who killed him – and probably wouldn't. There weren't any of the usual kinds of clues here. The Indios weren't a violent people and had the right to defend themselves from acts of violence in any manner they could. If someone is trying to kill you, you kill them first. Next case. Oh! By the way, don't ever move a body again! There will be consequences!

Clint shook his head and went to the pensión. He made one stop on the way to bring along a friend. The local medicine woman, Matilde. He asked about the visitors and was told they went to the breakfast place. One of them wasn't there. They thought he may have gotten up early and gone there.

Clint and Matilde went to the little café and saw the three standing on the porch. He introduced them to himself and Matilde. Matilde simply said, "No!" She smiled and walked away.

"I'm Maria Benito and these are my lawyers, Samuél and Ariela Acosta. My husband is somewhere around, Nesto Guevarra.

"What a strange woman! What was that about?"

"She said you aren't pregnant. She's the local medicine woman. She's never wrong."

"Not pregnant? Why would you care if I'm pregnant? It's not your concern."

"You told Ernesto you were raped and were pregnant by Arturo Jimenez.. It's become my business."

"It has? Why?"

"Because it caused your husband to be killed. He attacked Arturo with a knife. He came out second best in a two man contest."

She staggered and registered shock. It was a bit overdone.

"Don't say anything! My god!" Ariela yelled. Clint looked at her and caught the triumphant smirk on Maria's face through his phenomenal peripheral vision.

"None of you can leave the town until I've investigated," Clint said. "Seeing you've paid for a week, that shouldn't be a problem."

"No! We aren't involved!" Sam cried. "You can't say we killed anyone! You said it was in a knife fight! We had nothing to do with it!"

"Oh, you can answer a few questions honestly and maybe you can go. Maria can't."

"I can't? Really?" she seemed smug.

"Yep! Really!"

"You can't legally hold me and we all know it!" she spat.

"Yes, I can. This is the comarca. What's legal here and what's legal in the other parts of the country are different things in a lot of ways."

"Clint Faraday! I ... I have heard of you," Ariela said. "What questions do you have?"

"Have you ever gone anywhere before with Maria and spouse?"

"Well, no."

"Then why are you here? Nobody takes their lawyer on a vacation for no reason."

"That's confidential information," Sam warned.

"Very well, then. You can't leave because you offer no proof of innocence."

"But ... okay. We're here because Maria and Ernesto wanted to buy some land and open an exclusive hotel and restaurant. We were to handle the legal end."

"This is the comarca. You're lawyers. You're damned well aware that there won't be any hotel and restaurant here that's owned by any non-indigeno. You're lying. I said you could answer *honestly* and probably go."

"I'm not really married to Ernesto. Legally."

"Big deal! So what?"

"I planned to marry an Indigeno, then we could build the place."

"Oh? Be careful what you say!" Clint cautioned. "You come here to marry an Indigeno with your husband and the husband ends up dead.

"For your information, that wouldn't make any difference. You still couldn't buy land and build anything."

"No, but my *husband* could!"

"No, he couldn't. There's no ownership of land here.

"So you don't deny that you set something up to get rid of a inconvenient husband. Ever heard of conspiring to commit murder?"

"That doesn't come under those laws! There wasn't any conspiracy!" Sam cried.

"What laws? This is the comarca. It clearly comes under our laws. We don't have all those technicalities. We don't have any."

"Well, let's go somewhere else where we can discuss this in private," Maria suggested. "I'm sure we can work something out. There's a huge opportunity here to greatly help the people. We can bring in tourist money and supply jobs!"

"The very last thing we want here is more tourists."

"Maria!" Ariela said, sternly. "Mr. Faraday is worth many millions of dollars!"

Maria looked scared for the first time. She was warned that bribery wouldn't work with Clint Faraday!

"Okay, Faraday. You can claim conspiracy for Maria, but you can't for us. What's the deal?" Sam asked.

"Explain what you're really here for in a way that an idiot wouldn't see through."

"I don't think I can. I don't really know."

"Maria, I think I have a few very hard questions myself!" Ariela said. "Just exactly why in hell *are* we here?"

"But ... I thought I could marry an Indio and could build the hotel here!"

"And you brought your husband along so they could kill him? You *are* legally married to him. We're your lawyers! We would have to know that!"

"I didn't bring him here to get him killed! He knew I planned to open the resort and he knew the only way was for me to be married to an Indio! We were planning on getting a divorce anyway. He would claim that I was pregnant by Arturo and say he had to marry me. I can be married to two men on the comarca! I know that! Nesto would be a partner in the business.”

“Why attack him, then?” Ariela asked. “If he was only to convince him he should marry you, why attack him?”

“He wasn’t supposed to do that!”

“Did he think you were actually pregnant?” Clint asked.

“Uh, well, uh, he may have thought, I mean, maybe.”

“I see. That’s why he wanted a divorce.”

“He was sterile. Low sperm count. If I really was pregnant, he knew it wasn’t his. We weren’t getting along the past few months and I let him think I really was pregnant so he’d divorce me and I could come here and start something to make a living. He was mostly lazy and a layabout. I had to run the restaurant and support him. I thought this would be a way to force him to do something. He said he would agree to all of it and even helped design what I want to build here. Arturo was the best lover I ever had. We could make it work.”

“No, you couldn’t,” Clint replied. “There’s no way Arturo would marry you. He knows damned well there was no baby from him. He used neem. It’s proven to be a hundred percent effective as a contraceptive."

"I don't even know what that is. He didn't use anything that I saw."

"Mr. Faraday, we won't be needed here. We didn't know what the plan was. Maria only said she wanted to make a deal about using some land here. We would have told her no one owns land in the comarca and all deals were made with the council. We could advise. No more," Sam said. "We have to get back to our business. You said we could go if we answered your questions. Are there any more questions?"

"No."

"Then we can go?"

"No. I didn't say 'if you answered the questions.' I said if you answered them honestly."

"You don't believe we did?" Ariela asked.

"Not a chance!"

"Why?" Sam asked "I've answered everything you've asked!"

"And an idiot wouldn't accept your answers. Everyone on the streets in Panamá knows you can't ever own anything in the comarca. Your story is ludicrous.

"When I learn what you're really doing here I'll either say you can go or that you ain't going anywhere for awhile.

"You can go on with your vacation here. Make

arrangements to handle the body. I'll do a little investigating. Maybe you can go in a day or two. I want to go to my family for a couple hours, then I'll get information and decide what to do."

"How do we handle the body? What do we do?" Ariela asked.

"Discuss it with Doc. He's at the clinic and did a superficial autopsy. He obviously died of knife wounds. You can have the Indios make a casket or you can take him to Chiriqui Grande in a body bag."

"We'll get a casket. It's the least we can do," Sam said.

They went out. Clint sighed again and went home to his wife and kids for the afternoon.

Clint spent several hours making information requests on the net. No one had told the truth about anything. Whatever it was those lawyers were in it up to their necks.

Nito came in to ask what was going on. Santo told him some big man was stabbed by Arturo and that the turkey's wife set it up.

Six years old and he talked like he was thirty. He talked more like an adult since he was two.

"There's something strange going on with those lawyers and that woman," Clint explained. "She deliberately set up her husband to either get killed or to kill someone else and end up executed here on the comarca. That means whatever it is would get too much attention in the Panamanian cities.

"It's connected to this comarca. This area."

"Yeah. They get out in the parque when there's nobody close and read papers and show each other things.

"Dad, I'm going to the park with Bino. I think maybe they won't pay any attention to a couple of Indio kids who are playing there. They talk in English, but they haven't heard any of us kids talk in anything except dialect."

"Be damned careful, Son. That bitch set up her own husband to die."

"Yeah. I know." He went out. Nicole said she wanted to go with him. Tyna agreed, but only so long as there were several kids around. One loud yell of certain words and there would be twenty adults there in seconds.

Clint watched them go out and shook his head. He could picture anything like this happening in the cities or in the states. Five and six year old kids alone in the park. The parents a kilometer away.

On the comarca every adult was watching out for the children. It was part of the culture.

He went back to the computer to get the data about those people. The lawyers were semi-shady and had some connections in Mexico, Nicaragua and Colombia. It was suspected that they set up laundering deals. Ernesto had been in some trouble because of his violent nature. He had no convictions, though there had been more than twenty charges filed against him.

Mob. Same in the states. They owned judges and cops.

Maria's father was from Colombia. She had been legally married to Ernesto. Her ID name was Maria Laredo Benito de Guevarra. Her father had been Hernando Benito. He had died three years ago. No details. Cali, Colombia.

"No details" meant he was knocked over by one of the mobs or cartels. Too much of this had to do with mobs.

What could they want on the comarca? They had zero chance of setting anything up here.

Except maybe they wanted to try something just a bit different?

Clint told Tyna he had an idea and was going into town. She said to have the kids bring back hojaldra flour.

He took his boat. He saw Maria and lawyers in the park under a big ficus tree. They saw Clint and pointedly ignored him. Several children were playing close. The children all ran to hug him. He gave then each a cookie Tyna baked for them. He kept them in a container on the boat.

"They were talking about somebody called Berto or Sardina. They have some items missing from their luggage or something," Nito reported quickly, then the children all ran back into the park.

Clint hid a grin. If that trio knew anything about the Indio culture they would know that the park was very seldom used in the middle of the day, which was why they were meeting there, but that the children would be in school or at home doing chores. Indio children are part of a family and everyone in the family has things they do. They had a place in the family and community, unlike almost every other culture. They belonged somewhere and knew it. At three or four years they were learning responsibility. They were secure.

In short, if the children were there at that time of the day it was for a reason. The only reason had to be them.

Clint went to the community building to ask if anyone knew a Berto Sardinas.

"He's Cuna. He has a place around the point almost to the far end of the peninsula," Nando answered. "He might be alright. He's not popular. He's after money. Not many of us are."

"I hear there are a few Cuna here and some Ngobe and Guayme in the Cuna Yala," Clint said. "I want to know what in hell is going on!"

"They left their bags in the lobby while they went to get lunch. I took them behind the counter. I looked in them," Nando said. "I sort of forgot to put some of the papers back in."

Clint laughed. "What kind of papers?"

"Legal crap, I think. Contracts and maps. Sort of like those planos the government uses when you buy land outside."

"Can you bring them?"

"Okay." He went out. Five minutes later he brought in some papers. The maps or planos didn't show where the land was, but it showed deep water to the shore and a large flat area. If it was to scale, it included more than two hundred hectares.

The writing on the back of the elevation map said something undecipherable about Rigoberto Sardinas L.

Clint studied the papers a moment, then sat back. "So. They're stupid enough to think they could pull something like that off?"

"Yeah. Deep water and a place for an airstrip on the comarca where the regular police can't come and we can tell the EUA to kiss our rusty asses," Nando said. "So. What now?"

"Nando, they can't actually believe we'd permit anything like that!" Clint cried. "What the hell are they up to?"

"Panamanians would know that it could never happen. Maybe non-Panamanians wouldn't know that?"

"And get us involved with a drug cartel from Colombia. They walked all over the Indigenos there and think it can happen here. They'd set up a transfer point disguised as a tourist trap resort or something on that order. They'd be able to use that for laundering as well.

"When will Basilio get back?"

"Tomorrow morning."

"We can make a plan before the pigshit trio meet him. Maybe he'll be interested in making a deal so long as he gets, say, five million dollars a year with a deposit of, say, fifty million?"

Nando giggled. "That will confuse them no end! What happens to their plan to rip off a drug cartel, then?"

They did a high five.

<u>*Plans*</u>

"Basilio, this is what we figure is happening with that bunch," Clint explained. "It would be funny and fine with me if they hadn't tried to involve the people in the comarca. It could start a war among the drug people from Colombia. We sure as hell don't need that!"

He explained what they thought was happening. Basilio agreed that Clint had it figured pretty much as it should be planned. He'd make it a point to insert a worm into that papaya!

Clint had Nando, who was in on this, go to the hotel and tell the, as Clint called them, pigshit trio to come to the council building. Basilio was back and the case would be turned over to him. He was the jefe of the comarca on this side, meaning his word was law.

They came in acting a bit nervous. Clint told Basilio what they had on them in front of them so they could argue whatever parts needed argument. Basilio sat back and nodded, then thanked Clint and Nando for their help. He said any questions that came up he would send for them. Clint and Nando left them there with Basilio. They went out front and around to the side where they could hear everything that went on in the chamber.

Basilio: "... is a very serious thing, but it is not really the concern of the comarca, other than the fact you had him killed here. I wish you people would handle this kind of thing outside. Don't bring it here!

"Now. What is this silliness about you building a hotel here in Cusapín?"

Ariela: "That's what I think that Clint Faraday character didn't understand, though I think he deliberately didn't, if you get the drift. He doesn't like us because we're lawyers or something. We don't want to build it here, only on the peninsula on the other end. It won't interfere with Cusapín except to give some people jobs."

Basilio: "You can't own anything over there either. You can't build anything there if the council, me, doesn't say you can. It's true that it would give some jobs, but the people here don't want any jobs like that. They don't give a shit about your money, which is something you people can't seem to understand. They have no knowledge of the money society and don't have the desire to go anywhere or buy a lot of things that may make life easier, but have no real value."

Maria: "I'm sure that you, in your position as chief, have traveled a great way and know that it can make your life, as you say, easier and more pleasant. It can also pay for a lot of things that you need here. Medicine and that kind of thing."

Basilio: "Yes. I know there is some little use of money and I know how necessary it can be to your society. The problem about the crossover from one culture to another is the way money is used to dominate. In your culture you could offer a million dollars for the rights to the land, they would counter for two million, you would get it for a million and a half.

"Enough money to hold some power is one thing. Enough to get you enslaved by those with more is not the same basket of yuca."

Sam: "That's one point we can make. We can arrange for you to get enough that those people won't dare to try to pressure you with anything. I can say very clearly that our sponsors will wish to remain very low-key and will never make any demands. You will have enough that the more local money people won't dare to bother you.

"We would make a very large surety deposit and would guarantee to pay a good sum monthly or yearly or whatever.

"I was thinking on the lines of a deposit of ten or fifteen million dollars and a payment of a million dollars per month?"

Basilio: "That is something to consider, but not

in such piddling amounts. The initial deposit. Maybe a million per month after the first would be alright. I'll have to think about it for awhile.

"We have to resolve this killing thing. We can't do anything until that is done.

"I find that you probably did set your husband up to be killed. After reading the data Clint got on him he was doomed to die by such methods from ten years ago. I'm rather surprised he wasn't handled before this.

"I prefer to allow it to be handled outside. Your doing that here has placed a good man in a bad place. Arturo is not a violent person. You should have arranged that to be the ... well. Guevarra was involved with some unsavory people in his past. I imagine, knowing the type of person he was, he has or had something he was using to keep him safe from them. You will now have that. Should you attempt use of it against such people you will be handled much like he was.

"I will allow you to go after I inform them that Guevarra was handled by you. It then becomes your problem to protect yourself. That is the way of such things.

"The lawyers I will allow to leave also. Those people will have to consider whether or not you are now in possession of whatever you have. It should lead to an exciting if short life for you.

"You will remain here for three days. I will inform you when you may leave. Perhaps you will finish your vacation."

They said their goodbyes. Maria said to think carefully about what the comarca (Clint could picture the 'wink – wink') needs.

The pigshit trio headed straight for the park. Clint could see Nito and Jorge playing near the table under the tree.

"Well, your undercover operator will be right there!" Nando said. "I hope they do something really stupid now!"

"Yeah. Like get in touch with their boss and say they've got it as much as done so send them the money.

"I hope they discuss what they'll pay Basilio for his cooperation. We can up it a few million and keep them negotiating for a little while."

"Why?"

"Because that mob or drug cartel is going to get someone here fast with the money. I don't doubt that he'll have orders in case there's the kind of thing they plan going down."

"In which case they *will* be handled the way Guevarra was handled."

"You got it! But *not* on the comarca!"

They went to the cantina and had some coffee and hojaldres. Basilio came to join them. He asked how Clint was going to find out how much to hold them up for.

"Clint has a secret agent listening to them right now," Nando said. "We can let them tell us how much they'll pay, then you can demand more and negotiate it." He explained what Clint told him about the mob sending someone to guarantee the pigshit trio couldn't pull off what they were trying to pull off.

"Something they should have considered while making their original plan," Basilio said with a grin.

"I think the mob wants them to set something up they can use. They would have been knocked over in ten minutes once the deal was done," Clint argued.

"Which gives me an idea! I'll actually make a deal with them!" Basilio said.

"You will?" Nando asked.

"Yes. With *them*!"

"Ha! You think as sneaky as I do," Clint said. "Make the deal with them. Get your fifty million or whatever. They get knocked over. The mob has no deal. There was no legal ownership so the project gets shut down and everyone left lives happily ever after – except for the mob, who lost fifty or a hundred million in the deal!"

"And they have no recourse," Nando added.

They chatted for a few minutes. The pigshit trio broke up. Maria went toward the dock and the Acostas went to the hotel. As soon as they were inside Nito came to the cantina to report, "They called somebody in Medellin and talked about how they had it as much as done, but they would have to come up with about seventy five to a hundred million to consolidate the deal. The stuff Guevarra had seems to have disappeared. They could be sure the link with Flores wouldn't ever come out.

"The Maria woman said that they had to change their plans. This had to go down the way they said it would at first. They could collect a few million a year more by making it a legitimate deal.

"The man said nothing on Earth could make it a legitimate deal. They could get the few million like they planned from the deposit and a million or so a year from now until he dies of old age. That might be very nice.

"They want to meet with Basilio to find out how much to put the touch on for the deposit would be. They will also have to get in with you. You have a lot of influence. Maybe the fact it won't be in Cusapín will make a difference.

"I'm going home. I have to finish the garden while the moon's right."

"Thanks, Son. I'll make a detective out of you

yet!" He hugged Nito and he left.

"Maria's down by the dock. My boat's there. I'll let her convince me that the deal will be good for the comarca and everyone will get rich," Clint announced. "Basilio, say you've talked with the other jefes and you can finish a lot of things for sixty two million. That'll let them knock down thirteen million, an unlucky number for them. A million a month will keep the projects moving along after the initial construction and furnishing are done. When she's sufficiently shocked that it really is for the comarca and not for you you can point out that you have no personal need of money. Why in hell would you want more? Clint, your dear friend, will give you a million or two if you want it."

"You will?"

"Uh-huh. I have more than I'll ever need now!"

"You're already spending most of it on the people," Nando pointed out.

"Most of it, true. I still have a few million I don't need."

"Well, sixty two million, of which I'll issue you six million two hundred fifty thousand for your commission."

"Put it in the CJM fund."

The CJM fund was Clint, Judi and Manny. It was for building schools and clinics on the comarcas.

They joked about the money and about idiots who would try to rip off a drug cartel.

"They'd try to set it up so it would look like we didn't keep our end or something," Nando said. "Then they'd whine about how hard they worked and how they lost everything!"

"That would work with a hundred dollar loan maybe, but not with millions," Clint replied. "I think she's either stupid or crazy or both."

Clint went toward the dock. Maria was there looking out over the Caribbean. She greeted him and said she wanted to talk to him about a few things. She thought there was a major misunderstanding about what they wanted to do.

"If you'd just tell me the truth about anything once, I might believe that," Clint replied. "So you arranged for Ernesto to get offed. He's had it coming a long time. I checked on him. The only thing I have against that is that you involved Arturo and the comarca. He's a good man. We don't need the problems killing him here brings.

"That you want to build a fancy hotel here is understandable. It's a true paradise. The problem with that is that it wouldn't be paradise anymore with a bunch of arrogant obnoxious egocentric tourists making silly demands and treating my people like indentured servants."

"That's what I mean. We aren't planning for the

hotel to be here in Cusapín. It's to be on the other end of the peninsula tip. It's at least fifteen or twenty kilometers from here. We want it to be where it doesn't affect anyone here to any extent. We would possibly hire twenty or thirty people to run the place.

"I want you to understand that we didn't say the right things before. Basilio, who seems to be a very concerned person, understands and is considering letting us build the place if it will be that far away. We will do a lot for the comarca in other ways."

"It's Basilio's decision to make. He wouldn't do anything that might compromise anyone here. Understand that fully. If he finds you lied about anything, he'll rescind anything he's promised because it would be suspicious. You have to understand the way we think about such things. You lied to me so I'll never completely trust anything you say again. It will be the same with Basilio or any other Ngobe you ever deal with. Understand that or I can guarantee you'll come out third in a two horse race!"

"I think I do understand you. It's the way that business is done in the city. It won't work here."

"Which says a hell of a lot about how business is done anymore."

"Too true. I'll try to gain your confidence. I

really do think everyone can come out ahead in this."

"That would be a rarity! I have to get home. I'll probably see you later."

He got in the boat and went home. Let her think she'd convinced him of something. It would make them go ahead a bit faster.

That boat was headed for the rocks!

*Fishing Trip*

"I told them we wouldn't be interested. The projects we're working on here, our plans for the comarca, would cost more than sixty million dollars. I wasn't about to compromise the rules of the comarca for a thing that wouldn't accomplish everything the compromise was made *for*!" Basilio explained. "She whined and the lawyers whined. I told them that kind of beachfront property would sell for more than half a million per hectare on the market. If I understood where they wanted, that would be more than a hundred million so no more bullshit! The comarca needed sixty one million and nine hundred twenty two thousand to finish the important parts. Sixty two or take a hike!"

"Where did you get that figure?" Clint asked.

"I made it up."

"So they agreed on sixty two," Nando said with a smirk. "They still figure they'll get four million apiece with that, plus a lot of money for years."

"Maria said they would contact the partner and we could make a contract. I said they hadn't said anything about any partners before. The deal was off! It was already starting! Nobody tells anybody the whole truth and a bunch of exactly the kind of people we don't want here would be involved! Forget it!" Basilio replied. "Maria said that wasn't what she meant! She always said things in a way people got the wrong idea! They were partners in her other hotel is all! She would have them get the money together that was all! She should shut up and let the lawyers handle it! That's why they were there!

"I said we would make a contract. It would state exactly who was involved and there will be a clause that anyone else to get into the deal has to be approved by the council. Everything was to be handled only in the way the contract would state."

"Which will allow them to make a two hundred page contract that they can sneak things in on," Clint warned.

"No. I'll have you there as advisor because you know how business is done outside. You can explain about the contract law here, which there ain't none of, to them. You can explain what they're trying to say to me because I'm an ignorant clown who don't know from a cowflop."

Clint gave him the finger. They laughed.

"I'll have them come here at ten, more or less, to discuss how we'll handle it. If you can get Tyna to be here to record it on paper?"

"Tyna? Why?"

"Because of the way that Sam character looks at the girls here. I'll also have Arturo here to act as gofer."

Clint giggled. Basilio was going to show the pigshit trio a thing or two about sneaky business deals! Maria had already said Arturo was the best lover she ever had and Clint had seen the way Ariela had sized him up and licked her lips. Sam couldn't get his eyes off of the pretty girls. Tyna was a knockout.

"A little distraction can't hurt anything!" Clint agreed.

He called Tyna and said to put on that tight sun dress she wore when they were out in the boat. She asked why and he said he'd pick her up in the boat in a few minutes. She was going to be the recording secretary for the council.

"Basilio doesn't need any ... oh! That Sam character is going to be there. Nilda and Gloria say he's always staring at them like they were big helados. It will be fun!"

Clint went to the boat and got her. She had on a shapeless over-large traditional dress. He didn't say anything. He figured she knew what she was doing. She had a sort of Homburg hat with her hair under it.

"You look more like Peru!" Clint charged. She

giggled.

They went back. She went to Jessie's place. They would send for her when everyone was there.

Clint was dying of curiosity, but determined not to say anything. Arturo came and they got their heads together.

"Don't turn this into a comedy act!" Clint warned. They laughed.

Basilio had a boy come to ask Clint to come to the council house. He was almost there when a fast cigarette boat came to the dock. Two big men in suits got off.

Ring them into the meeting and it would be over before it started! Basilio had warned them about bringing anyone else into the deal.

They headed for the hotel. One took out a celular and made a call.

Clint stepped into the council house as Sam answered his phone. Clint hid a grin.

"We're in a business meeting right now. I'll talk to you when we're through. We can go on our *fishing trip* this afternoon. After all, that's why you're here! Sorry the business came up just now, but that's how it goes."

"Yes, true. The fishing has been very good lately. The big ones are running."

"That wouldn't be a good idea.."

"No! The fish won't bite if there are too many boats in the area!"

"Fine! I'll see you in a bit." He rang off. "Some friends from, er, Costa Rica. Came for a fishing trip."

"I saw a boat coming to the dock," Clint said. "There's not a lot of room for fishing in those cigarette boats, but everyone to their own taste."

"I've sent a boy to bring Tyna to act as secretary and Arturo to be here to bring anything else we may need. I think coffee and some hojaldres?" Basilio said. "Everyone take a seat, please."

"Why are you here, Mr. Faraday?" Ariela asked.

"I've asked that he be here because he speaks much better Spanish than do I," Basilio replied. "He also knows something of business and about contracts, both those of the comarca and those of the outside."

Tyna came into the house and was introduced. Basilio looked a question at Clint, who shrugged. She put a pad and some pens on the table and took off the hat, letting her waist-length shiny black hair fall and shaking it. Sam's eyes seemed to almost be ready to pop out of his head.

She put the hat on a rack by the door and reached to undo the outer dress. She slipped out of it, smiled at everyone, and hung it on the rack.

"It's needed in the sunlight outside, but there's

no sun inside," she explained, innocently. Sam was actually gasping. Ariela looked like she could strangle him. Tyna was a spectacular beauty. "Where should I sit? At the table or at the little desk? Is this official?"

"The desk, close to that side, please," Basilio answered. "This is partly official."

Sam jumped up and pulled the small desk to exactly opposite where he was sitting. Tyna smiled and said, "Muchas gracias!" Clint glanced at Basilio, who was trying not to show how much he was laughing inside.

"If we will all now take our seats?" Basilio requested.

"Yes! Do!" Ariela snapped.

The door opened and Arturo came in wearing a brief bathing suit and nothing more. "Do you want anything?" he asked.

"Oh, yeah!" Maria cried, then caught herself. "I could use some hot black coffee and a sweet or something."

"I could use a sweet or two myself," Ariela said. "Café con leche."

"Coffee and hojaldres," Clint ordered. "Are things better now, Arturo?"

"Fine, Clint. Hi, Tyna!"

"Chicha. Guanabana if there's any prepared," Basilio ordered. "Shall we get a basic idea of what we want to accomplish here?

"You will want a contract. That's business. We will keep it very simple. That is the only way to avoid silly arguments later.

"Tyna, make a list of what we request be in the contract if you will?

"I will start by saying this is to be a contract among the three people in this room who wish to establish a business on the north portion of the peninsula and the comarca. Others such as Clint, you, and Arturo are here from duty and are no part of the contract except as testigos.

"If we can agree to that?"

"We represent a corporation," Sam suggested. "Make it between the corporation and the comarca."

"We'll want to give you these planos. It's the property that's under discussion and the holder at this time has signed the contract with us that we may do this," Ariela said, handing Basilio a folder of planos. "We didn't want any questions with the comarca, even though we know the land isn't owned by individuals here. We want no future animosity because someone thinks we are trying to dispossess them."

"There are no corporations on the comarca. All contracts include only the named entities," Clint said. "You can make any deals with corporations for use on the outside and among yourselves, but the corporation has no meaning here."

"Oh! Well, I don't see...." Sam began. Tyna dropped a pencil and leaned over to pick it up. She smiled at Sam, whose eyes were almost bugging out again. "Uh. Yes," he finished.

"I don't think, well, if that's how...." Maria said.

"We can work something out to mutual agreement," Ariela stated. "This session should be basic. Details can be added when we have a plan. We would waste the whole day arguing every fine point.

"I mean, the corporation would just be us so what's the difference?

"I think lawyering like in the system outside just seems silliness here. A contract that's, as friend Basilio suggested earlier – basic – is all we need. The important thing is to get this project started!"

"I agree with that," Clint said. "I know from experience that this project would take a year or more to even begin outside. There would be a hundred meetings, each of which would add a clause to the contract, which would be twenty to fifty pages of contradictions.

"Here, say what you have to say in the shortest way you can. Two pages is a long contract. It can be done today and you can start construction tomorrow.

"Remember that you're part of the corporation or whatever here and now. You're not going to get an extra thousand dollars for each delay you can cause. You can't make side deals or sell-out with any of the opposing lawyers. There ain't any opposing lawyers.

"Just say for X amount of dollars the comarca grants the named persons to utilize the described property for these purposes and that the contract is valid for the times and in the terms stated. You don't have to say a dock of exactly fifty meters by four meters on the GPS location blah, blah, blah. That doesn't mean anything here."

"Clint, how would you suggest we word a contract so it will be valid both on the outside and here?" Basilio asked.

"Keep it simple. We, the named persons, enter into a legal contract as of this date. The contract is for use of the property located wherever and of such size. Any other person to be added must meet with approval of all parties.

"You make a standard plano and put a copy with the contract. Those Ariela brought will do. We already have them.

"The named may construct docks, buildings, roads and other services according to the attached blueprints or as agreed in separate dealings.

"The named persons enjoin this contract legally

upon placing X dollars into the hands of the comarca representative. Basilio will be that.

"A continuing use fee of X dollars per month or year or whatever will also be placed into the representative's hands at times stated for the term of this contract.

"Agreed and signed as of this date. Testigos. Comarca authority. Contract members.

"Let's go have a beer to celebrate."

"Do you want that written in the contract?" Tyna asked innocently.

Everyone laughed. Basilio said, "Why not? A binder of sorts!"

They all congratulated each other hardily. Arturo brought the snacks and coffee, including himself and Tyna in it. They sat around the table and chatted. They would be back in one hour for Tyna to show them the basic contract they would make. They could add whatever at that time and  meet either later or tomorrow for the signing and transfer of funds.

"Oh! I suppose we should make it tomorrow. You have that fishing trip this afternoon," Clint said.

"I can use this for an excuse to not go. They can go fish by themselves," Sam replied. "They're just business acquaintances. They'll understand that business comes first.

"Basilio, I'll arrange for the cash to be delivered right away. It will be cash because it's unreported funds if you know what I mean. You won't have trouble with that. You don't have to explain to a lot of government idiots where and why you got the money."

"Yes. That will do. I know a laundering scheme when I see it. I'm not so unsophisticated as you may think."

Maria laughed. "I thought you were on to us from the first! Like you say, it doesn't make any difference to you. You don't have to explain where comarca money came from."

"There's one very definite thing," Clint warned. "There will be *no* funny money brought here."

"That would void the contract," Basilio said. "Counterfeit has no value, thus the amount wouldn't be paid, would it? I don't think these people are stupid enough to do anything like that."

They agreed to come back in an hour. Everyone except Basilio, Tyna and Clint left.

Tyna said she had a rough outline of the contract. She would print it out when she had it like they wanted it. It was simple and would cover everything.

Basilio and Clint went to the dock to look over the cigarette boat. One of the men was there. He introduced himself as William Salardos. He said he was there to go fishing.

"In a suit?" Basilio asked. "And in that boat?"

"Er."

"We know they're wanting to launder money. You don't have to play silly games," Clint said. "It's all legal on the comarca and it'll get a lot of our projects paid for. Big fucking deal!"

Salardos laughed. "Ariela said that you weren't fooled. She said that the jefe here is probably smarter than our whole bunch combined.

"We will build the hotel and that crap."

"Of course. It couldn't continue without that. You don't have to show me anything, but you will have to show the outside government something if you ever want any of the money to leave the comarca," Basilio said.

"You brought the seventy five million?" Clint asked.

"Eighty five, but we expected that. It's part of the business.

"Where do you want me to put it?"

"Wait until the contract is signed," Basilio replied. "We keep it totally legal as to comarca law. We never want a question about us keeping the contract word for word."

"Okay. Then where?"

"I haven't thought about it. I guess the council house?"

"You can deposit it in the comarca account in a couple of days," Clint suggested. "We don't want it here. Our people wouldn't take it except for food or whatever. The tourists would scheme and kill each other to get it. Give everybody in town a hundred dollars or something for a joke. Take it to Buabidi and put it in the bank."

"Okay. We can do that," Basilio said.

"Jesus Cristo! Eighty five million in cash and you just leave it on the table in the council house?! I hope you have good locks!"

"There are no locks on the council house. It belongs to the comarca. We wouldn't lock our people from their own property!" Basilio stated positively.

"I wish I could start over and live in a place like this," Salardos said. "Money, over a certain amount, doesn't mean anything."

"Wisdom comes too late in life for most of us," Basilio replied.

They chatted a bit, then went to walk on the beach, then went back to the council house.

"Let's see," Sam said. "The aforenamed ... sixty two million ... plano attached ... no others ... it's what we talked about. Simple and exact. I don't see where we need any changes." He handed it to Ariela.

"Hm. What if we ... by mutual agreement ... it's

there.

"Less than a page and everything's covered! You would put lawyers out of business in a day here!" She handed it to Maria.

"I think this is iron-clad! We really can start construction tomorrow! Literally!

"Well, Basilio. We can arrange for the money to be here this afternoon. This is a done deal!"

"Salardos is putting the money right here in the council house as soon as we sign," Basilio said.

"He! Er, that is, we didn't...!" Sam cried.

"I'm not stupid. What other reason could there be for that silly boat coming here? Fishing? In a cigarette boat? In business suits? Gimme a break, as Clint says. We talked with him. I told him to put the money here."

"Er, there are some expenses included. We have to take those out," Maria said.

"Yes. Eighty five million dollars? That's a good commission."

Maria looked wary, then laughed. "We didn't fool you for a second did we? We think we're being clever, but we're being stupid.

"How much?"

"How much for what?"

"To not say anything about the commission."

"I don't care. The comarca gets what was agreed. You can do what you like with the rest."

"Then lets get this boat in the water!" She signed the contract and handed it to Sam. He signed and handed it to Ariela. She signed and handed it to Basilio, who did the same and handed it to Tyna, who handed it to Clint.

"Tyna, make everybody a copy and file this, please," Basilio said. "Now for that final clause!"

"Yeah! It really does say we'll celebrate with a beer!" Sam said.

They got their copies and headed for the cantina. They chatted for awhile, then the pigshit trio headed for their hotel. They would ride back to Chiriqui Grande in the cigarette boat. They already had their "commission" in their luggage.

Basilio had Clint call for the chopper he used at times. They loaded the money onto it and Basilio made out a deposit slip. Arturo and Nando would take it to Buabidi for deposit to the comarca account.

Clint and Tyna went home. Nito greeted them. Nicole had cooked a delicious lobster chowder for dinner.

All-in-all, a pretty good day!

<u>*And Then....*</u>

"Clint? Tonio here," greeted Clint as he laid on his hammock with Nicole and Nito before turning in for the night.

"Yo! Que pasa?"

"You made some kind of business deal with some lawyers named Acosta and a woman called Maria Guevarra?

"No. Basilio did. A money laundering thing."

"Money laundering? And you tell me, the police, about it?"

"It's on the comarca. We don't give a shit so long as we get ours. We don't have to explain where we got the money."

"Clint! Don't get involved in laundering!"

"We're not. The pigshit trio paid for use of some land. They're double-dealing the cartels. They won't be around long."

"The Acostas aren't around any longer already."

"Already? Oh? The lovely Maria wasn't hit?"

"She was still in the hotel. The Acostas got into their fancy new BMW and turned the ignition. Boom!"

"Was she supposed to be with them?"

"Probably. They went out while she paid the hotel bill. I guess he started the car to run the air conditioning."

"Shit! Did she do it or did they?"

"They?"

"The two in the cigarette boat who were from the cartel to deliver the cash."

"I heard about that boat. It brought them. They had left some things at the hotel and had left the car in the lockup there."

"Did Maria have her luggage in the car?"

"No. It was there by the desk."

"Then she did it. Check her luggage."

"For?"

"About twenty million dollars."

There was a silence.

"You still there?"

"Yeah. I was trying to think of a way that a million or so could disappear between the hotel and here. It's only two damned blocks!

"How do we pin it on her?"

"Was there any money found inside the car? In their luggage?"

"I don't know yet."

"If she has that much and they didn't have much it's because she stole it from them, then killed them to stop anybody from making a claim. It's the only way it figures. We have the contract that makes them equal partners in a business. She wouldn't have it all.

"We have one problem. When did she have the time to hook up a bomb?"

"I'll have to try to find out. By what I saw the bomb was in the car. In the back seat. A plastic explosive."

"Then it was easy. All you have to establish is whether she had access to the car after they arrived there and before the Acostas went to it."

"Ten minutes. I'm by the lockup. You can listen and maybe ask a question or two. Jorge Silas is attendant. This is on speaker now.

"Jorge, did anyone come to this car in the past hour and a half?"

"Si. The other lady. She said she had a package for in the car."

"So she was in the car for how long?"

"Maybe five minutes. I saw her leaving about then. She still had the package. I didn't think about it then."

"Thank you. Any questions, Clint?"

"What size was the package?"

"Maybe like a box. Maybe fifty centimeters by thirty centimeters by twenty centimeters."

"Just about right. Thanks.

"Anything like that in her luggage, Tonio?"

"Uh-huh. How did she work the bomb?"

"She took a bit of plastic explosive and wired it to the air conditioner switch. Two minutes. Start the car and turn on the air. Boom!"

"Okay. I'll pick her up and inspect her luggage. If it's there, she's down for the count."

"Let me know what happens. She's involved in actions that would bring bad publicity to the comarca. All contracts are void."

"I don't know what the hell you're talking about, but that's nothing new."


"Clint? She didn't have the money in her luggage."

"Shit!"

"She had it at the dock in a locker. She was seen going there just after going to the car. Almost across the street. It took a couple of minutes. Thought you'd like to know."

"Thanks."

Clint sighed and suggested he and Tyna go to bed. They had just finished preparing and getting into bed when the phone buzzed again. Clint swore and answered.

"Clint? The Maria woman?"

"What about her, Tonio?"

"It seems she committed suicide in her cell."

"Bullshit!"

"I agree, but it looks like it.

"Is that something to do with the money? With where she got it?"

"More how she got it, but yes."

"Mob?"

"Cartel."

"Then it's suicide. She strangled herself with her blouse."

"Talk about bullshit! How in holy hell do you strangle yourself?"

"Well, it looks like it and no one else was back there except earlier. The woman from her hotel came to see that she was alright and to get a lawyer for her if she wanted. Maybe if Bino hadn't gotten that long call from some woman who demanded he stop a fight at the bar that caused him to leave for about ten minutes he would have been able to stop the suicide.

"He's a rookie, Clint. He went over to the bar and it was only a couple of drunk men yelling at each other about a woman. He told them to shut up or they'd sit in a cell for the night. They shut up. He thought it was a bit easy."

"Did you talk to the men?"

"No. They were long gone. The bartender said something about a woman who came to the door and looked in. It seemed she slipped back out, but they saw her there. Both of them had a date or something.

"A setup. They aren't around anymore. It was suicide because she crossed those people, Clint."

"Agreed. Good night."

Clint answered the call from Basilio and said he'd be right there. The men in the cigarette boat were back. He got in his boat and headed for the town dock. Salardos and a man named Benicio Cauchero were there, arguing with Basilio.

"Clint, these people say they have a contract to use the property that the Guevarra woman has a contract to use. I'm afraid they don't make much sense. They say the national law says they can use it or something. They don't understand that the national law isn't the same as comarca law, so that isn't true.

"Maybe you can find what they want?"

Cauchero handed Clint a copy of the contract with Maria and the Acostas. Clint shrugged.

"They were partners with us. We want to go ahead with the project," Cauchero said.

"I have a question or two, but first, you aren't mentioned in this contract. It states very plainly that only those named and signing were involved.

"Second, how did you get this copy? They each had their copy when they left here.

"Third, how do you know they're all dead?

"I think Maria killed the Acostas, but someone from your little group knocked her over. That had to be planned all along or you wouldn't have had that woman who posed as someone from her hotel in Chiriqui Grande.

"You might have gotten by if she was still alive. There would be the one person who could act within the contract.

"How did you fuck up that bad?"

"They said it was settled, that we were in," Salardos said. "Nito thinks they made a deal on the side and this was just for show. I tried to tell him that couldn't happen with you.

"We expected her to get rid of the Acostas. There are some things about her past you don't know. She's done it before. She worked with some people from the old cartels.

"Can we make a deal with you?"

"If it's just the laundering part, I think so, but with some very clear understandings of how things will go down. With running, no. Period."

"What running!?" Cauchero demanded.

"Mow, let's see. A deep water access. An airstrip. This isolated location inside the comarca. You running around in a boat with four two fifty horse engines.

"DUH!"

"That's the important part of the equation,"

Salardos said. "We can make the laundering deal with any number of places. It's already operating in another comarca."

"Can't do it. I won't subject my people to what that brings," Basilio cautioned. "Please don't even discuss that more. It will not happen."

"We'll see! You don't think I'm going to just let you take me for eighty five million dollars and do nothing about it, do you? I'll bring my people here and teach...." Cauchero snarled.

"Shut the fuck up, dickhead!" Salardos snapped. "You're just a flunky, same as me. It didn't cost you anything. Paulo's going to be very interested in learning that it's your group and that you make threats in his name."

"He's exactly the type why we won't allow running here," Basilio said, calmly. "You can tell Paulo he demonstrated what we feared was true.

"As to the eighty five million, Maria and friends ripped you off. We simply made a contract with them. We kept and would have kept the agreements exactly."

"Which one of you arranged for the demise of Maria? – like I couldn't figure that!" Clint asked. "All you had to do was read the contract and you would have seen that was the stupidest thing you could possibly have done. It was beyond stupid!"

"You wouldn't have allowed the running

anyhow," Salardos said.

"With her. She would have kept it very low-key. She knew the limits. She knew it could work if she never did anything to involve more than you. Never any of my people," Clint explained. "I could keep her in line. Such as your buddy here would never even come here.

"He hasn't been here more than an hour and is already making threats and demands. No way!

"You, we might work okay with. His type are inevitable now. I have to agree with Basilio. No way!"

"It's a writeoff. A hundred mil isn't much to Paulo and he knows what went down.

"C'mon, Nito. Let's get out of here and back to some place we can understand."

"You don't really think I'm going to just walk away from eighty million dollars, do you?" he screeched.

"Why not?" Clint asked. "It's not your – or were you planning to steal a few million of it yourself?

"Paulo will consider it a business expense."

"Fuck! You don't even know who Paulo is!" Cauchero accused.

"Paulo Machado? I don't?" Clint asked. He had heard that name among the major cartel bosses. Salardos looked surprised at that.

"You knew who you were dealing with and went

ahead with it?"

"Yes. We were dealing with the pigshit trio. I naturally checked."

Salardos laughed. "Pigshit trio! I like that!

"C'mon, Nito. He's been ahead of us from the get-go. If he's not worried about Paulo, I won't be.

"It's interesting. He has things figured really close. Were you planning to knock down a few million on Paulo? Is that why you're so set on being a badass.

"Clint, one favor?"

"Such as?"

"I didn't mention any Machado. Neither did dickhead."

"Mitch who?"

"Thanks. I checked on you. Your word's your life. You also have quite a few million of your own. That will really go to the comarca won't it?"

"Every centavo. It really will help. We can build a big central hospital in Buabidi. That's what Basilio has in mind."

"I hope I meet you again someday in better circumstances, as they say. I think you'd be a good drinking buddy."

"It could happen!"

"So long and good fortune, Basilio. I think I respect you as much as anyone I've ever met."

Basilio answered, "I think I like you, too. Good fortune and bien viaje!"

Cauchero started to protest. Salardos shoved him into the boat. He waved and they pulled away from the dock.

"Salardos will return," Basilio decided.

"As a guest," Clint agreed. "I'll go back to the family. I don't think we'll have anymore trouble from that bunch."

He got in his boat and left. He went to his dock and tied up to it. Nito, Nicole and Tyna were swimming close. They had a basket with a large langosta in it.

"You aren't getting tired of lobster are you?" Tyna asked.

"It's not the kind of thing it's easy to get tired of," Clint replied. He dove into the water and joined his family to play and tease awhile, then they went to rinse in the shower on the dock and laid there to dry.

"Dad," Nito said, "I didn't get to tell you about what that Maria woman said on her celular when they were going to get in that fast boat.

"She was talking to someone she called Belinda and said the deal was done and that she'd see her in Chiriqui Grande in a couple of hours and to have the stuff ready to put in the car. She had worked it so her name didn't even get mentioned.

She could say she was from the hotel and was there to help. Somebody named Paulo would never be mentioned and that she worked for him wouldn't. She wouldn't need the stuff anymore and had called and had it erased."

Clint shook his head. He did again. Tyna asked what that was for.

"The lovely Maria had something on Paulo that was keeping her safe. The Belinda woman had worked for Paulo and was working with Maria to doublecross him. She felt she had made a deal where she wouldn't have to use whatever it was. She didn't consider it was also why Belinda was going along with her. It was something that could get Belinda's ass in a crack!

"She made the mistake of telling Belinda the evidence was erased. Belinda wasn't in a position of having to scheme with her anymore and resented her. She got rid of the Acostas with Belinda's help. Now she was the only thing between her and freedom. Exit Maria."

"Such people!" Tyna said. Clint had to agree.

About ten minutes later Clint's phone rang. It was Salardos.

"Clint? Benito didn't hit Maria."

"I know."

C. D. Moulton's works are available on most major outlets as printed or e-books. CD writes the CD Grimes, PI, mysteries, the Det. Lt. Nick Storie mysteries, the Clint Faraday mysteries, the Flight of the Maita science fiction series, books on orchid culture and many others of many types. Mystery, adventure, intrigue, science fiction, humor, fantasy, paranormal, mild erotica, and factual.

www.ingramcontent.com/pod-product-compliance
Lightning Source LLC
Chambersburg PA
CBHW072205150726
48002CB00014B/1379